THE
ENEMY IN
THE MIRROR

SANDRA MILLER

THE ENEMY IN THE MIRROR

A Novella

By

Sandra Miller

The Enemy in the Mirror
Published by Onda Mountain Books

Cover Design by Sandra Miller

Cover Art
© Bblood | Dreamstime.com
© Michel Van Loon | Dreamstime.com
© Rck953 | Dreamstime.com

Copyright © 2010 by Sandra Miller.

This is a work of fiction. Names, characters, places and incidents either are the product of the author's imagination or are used fictitiously, and any resemblance to any actual persons, living or dead, events, or locales is entirely coincidental.

Discover other titles by Sandra Miller at
www.sandra-miller.com

Until I rounded the corner of the engineering building and saw the rocket chair hovering in the university courtyard, I guess I thought I was used to the idea of Allacore attacks. I thought, like so many around me, that I knew everything there was to know about them. But an Allacore too lazy to fly? I despised them, but this was a new low even for them. This Allacore must have stood over ten feet tall--if she ever got out of that flying chair of hers long enough to stand. Her wings must have been curled against her back, because I couldn't see any evidence of them at all. The splintered ragged tips of her unkempt talons jutted out even when they were retracted. Her close-cropped white hair looked like it hadn't been washed in weeks. Their snowy white wing feathers and their equally white hair were the most attractive features Allacores had, if the word attractive could even be used, but on her neither were visible. Her gold metal armor must have been a sight to behold when it was new. At this point, though, it was dingy and pitted, and only added to her overall impression of disrepair.

Allacore. Just the name was enough to make my skin crawl, and here was one in my hometown! I stood there in shock as she hovered over the university path, herding students just like me into the holding cells that had been set up on the grass. We were out of her direct line of sight for the moment, but all too soon I knew we would be following our glassy-eyed peers into those dismal little cells. The Allacore mind-control devices were efficient. We were only spared the effect because we had not been there when she fired it. But she could handle the two of us easily enough. After that, who knew? Hard labor in their factories, servitude in their homes, forced indenture on their small attack ships--any of a hundred unpleasant fates could await this newest group of prisoners once they were taken back to the enormous generation ship that had brought the Allacore here, the generation ship that even now orbited Earth.

I glanced at Trevyn standing there beside me, his face a picture of shock as he surveyed the scene playing in front of us, fresh out of a nightmare. Of course we had all heard about the Allacore raids, but who expected them this far inland, here in the middle of nowhere?

Before I had recovered my wits, Trevyn had let go of my hand and was striding purposefully toward the Allacore's hovering chair. I should have guessed he would do something of the sort-- Trevyn never could stand by and watch injustice. The battle may have been doomed, but he was determined to fight it, even unarmed. He would not go quietly, like the groups of hypnotized students around him.

"Commander! I demand that you cease this at once!" Trevyn's

voice rang off the nearby buildings. I found time to wonder how he had known the Allacore's rank--I should have guessed that politically minded Trevyn would have been studying the Allacore raids much more intensively than I.

The rockets under the Allacore's chair glowed red as she swiveled it around to face Trevyn--and me behind him. I shivered under that emotionless stare; she regarded us as if we were so many bugs. "You demand?" Her voice grated like ground glass crunching under boots. "You? Who are you to demand anything of me?"

"I am Trevyn Blaine, and I am a citizen of this free country, a country which does not allow the sort of acts you are committing here." I stood as if my feet were rooted to the spot, horrified. *Oh, please God, don't let her kill him,* I implored in my mind.

The Allacore's face clouded with rage. "Filthy human!" she spat. "I'll teach you some manners, you rude little bastard." Her ragged talons were fully extended now, and she reached for the directional control on her chair.

The tension building in me was suddenly too much to bear. The capture of hundreds of students shocked me, but did not spur me to action; my own death I could have accepted with hardly a protest. But when she turned against Trevyn I could stand there no longer. Acting completely out of an instinct I hadn't known I possessed, I balled my right hand into a fist and held it high over my head. "Enough!" I cried, and against her will the Allacore found her attention pulled from Trevyn and focused entirely on me.

"Enough?" Her tone was syrupy sweet. Her broken, yellowed teeth flashed at me as she smiled a condescending smile. "Enough of what, human? I haven't yet begun!"

If she had dropped her superiority attitude and really looked at me, she would have noticed the bright yellow light streaming from beneath my curled fingers, pouring from between my knuckles. But she didn't see, and I held my hand clenched in that fist for a moment longer. "I command you to stop!" I shrieked, and to my surprise my voice echoed and re-echoed, even stronger than Trevyn's had a moment before. Before the Allacore commander recovered from her surprise, I pulled back my arm and flung it out towards her, opening my hand. The ball of light that left my grasp was like a miniature sun, racing toward her too fast for the eye to follow. It crashed into her chair and sent it reeling, casting scorch marks deep into her battered armor.

If I could have kept my wits about me, I would have grabbed Trevyn and run right then. But I was stunned, absolutely unable to believe what I had just done. I stood there gaping in disbelief while she brought her runaway chair under control and veered back toward me, whipping out a strange device that resembled a telescope. "So we have a powerful little monster here," she grated. "So this trip will be considerably more worthwhile than I had imagined. Your power will benefit me greatly, human." She leveled the telescope-thing at me, and it began to hum.

It was plain from her words that the thing was stealing whatever strange power I had, but I felt as though it was leeching all my energy. My knees buckled and I fell onto the sidewalk, marshaling everything I had for one last strike. This time when I flung out my shaking hand, no miniature sun burst forth. The Allacore laughed an ungodly laugh when she saw the wispy stream of light that issued from my palm--but she stopped laughing when the tendril of light wrapped itself around her telescope-thing and snatched it from her grasp. I jerked my hand to my chest, and the light recoiled, pulling the telescope-thing into my palm with a satisfying slap. "No, Allacore," I told her, leveling the device at her, "I think it is your power that will benefit me." The device hummed louder than before, and she began to shriek.

I was bursting with energy. I could have run a marathon, and I suppose at that point I should have stopped. I was past caring about the welfare of this despicable Allacore, though, and I noticed that her shrieks had gotten the attention of the masses of students around me. As she weakened, they came forth from the cells, broke out of the mindless lines they had been herded into, and encouraged by this, I held the device steady. The hum was deafening now, drowning out the Allacore's unholy screams. The device was shaking so hard that I needed both hands to hold it.

All at once the Allacore was silent. Her body seemed to crumble, to collapse in on itself--and then she was gone. The chair crashed to the ground and lay still, sitting at a sharp, broken angle. On the grassy field where hundreds of people had been prisoners only moments before there was silence, and then the cheering started. Grateful students surged out of the holding cells and toward me, cheering their happiness, their thanks. I knelt panting there on the path, the telescope-thing hanging useless from my hand, stunned. It was Trevyn who reached me first, Trevyn who pulled me to my feet and started dragging me away from the crowd. "We have got to get you out of here, Ellane!" he shouted over the noise, and the alarm in his tone brought me back to my senses. Without questioning why, I ran with him, following him away from the university campus and the masses of students who had so narrowly avoided capture.

*****

Trevyn secured the door, fastening the lock in the knob, the

9

deadbolt, and the chain lock before he turned to regard me where I sat shaking on his couch. It was all too much, it had all happened too fast, and the shock of it was threatening to overcome me. The look Trevyn gave me as he approached said I had no time for that.

"You can go lie down and recover in a few minutes," he told me, sitting down next to me. "Right now I need to talk to you. The situation is very serious. What happened back there?"

"What do you mean, what happened back there?" I said indignantly, frightened by his grave tone and offended by his manner. "You played hero with an Allacore commander, that's what happened back there. And she was going to kill you for it."

"Probably," he agreed, with a calmness that frightened me further. "In the end it wouldn't have mattered. Lots of people would have died there, one way or another. I might have bought them some time, maybe time enough for some of them to escape."

"You would have bought them nothing," I said sourly. "You saw them; they were like sheep. They would never have thought to run. And you would have been dead. But they didn't have to run, and you didn't have to die. Why is that so serious?"

"Oh, Ellane," he sighed, taking my hand, "that is so typical of you. You think so much about some things, and then not at all about others. Right now all of those people are very grateful for what you did. They'll go home and they'll tell their families and friends about their miraculous savior. But in a day or two--or less--that will fade. Human nature is strange. They won't remember the terror of their capture, or the danger they were in, or any of that. What they will remember is you, and the impossible things you did today. The Allacore commander is gone. They will never have to deal with her again. But you are still here, and still among them. Do you think, after what they saw today, they will ever think of you as normal again?"

I sat there dumbfounded as his words sank in. "I'm not normal," I said finally, realizing it for the first time. I met his eyes, and they were sad eyes. "What can I do?"

"I don't know," he said heavily. "But I do know you shouldn't go back to your place. There was probably no one in that crowd who knew you, but you shouldn't take that chance. Stay here."

"But--what about you? You're student body president. Almost all of them knew who you were."

"Undoubtedly. But then, I wasn't the one who fought an Allacore with balls of light. I'm sure I will be asked about you. For your protection, I think I'm going to have to lie. I'll tell them I have no idea who you were. In their state, I doubt any of them saw us walk up together."

I frowned. "But if they find me staying here?"

"How? They will need a search warrant to get in, and if they get one, we'll get you out of here before they come to serve it. I can protect you, Ellane, but you're going to have to trust me."

"I trust you completely," I told him, and he squeezed my hand.

"Then tell me what that was earlier."

"I don't know, and that's the God's honest truth. I've never done anything like that before--I never knew I could. I only knew I couldn't let her kill you. I had to stop her. And I did."

"Yes, you did." He sighed, and patted my hand. "You'd better go rest now. You look like you need it. Whatever that was, it had to be a strain." He stood up and led me down the short hallway, into what was apparently the apartment's second bedroom. The double bed must have had an extra mattress on it, as tall as it was, and the bedspread and curtains were pastels. I glanced at him, and he flushed. "Well, I had intended on asking you to move in at some point," he said uncomfortably. "I just

11

didn't realize it would be like this."

I hugged him hard. "Thank you, Trevyn." His shirt muffled my voice.

"You're very welcome, of course." He suddenly stepped back from me. "Now get some rest. I'm serious about that."

"Yes, sir." I saluted facetiously as he closed the door behind him.

*****

So that was how I came to be living with Trevyn Blaine. As he predicted, there was a hostile backlash against my actions, which I thought was completely insane. Where would all those angry people have been if I hadn't done what I had? Enslaved? In medical experiments? Dead?

It didn't seem to matter. Overnight, Trevyn became the hero of the campus, the one who had stood fast and saved them all from the Allacore commander. According to popular opinion, he had saved them from me as well, running me off before I could do them harm. I never left the apartment, but Trevyn brought home the papers. The editorials burned off the pages. I sighed and shook my head; what else could I do? Human nature was what it was, and if Trevyn tried to explain what had happened, they would have turned on him as well.

So I hid out in the apartment, and I stopped attending my classes, and I never went out into the world for a moment. I stayed in my room--and I practiced. What had come so easily in the high emotion of battle was hard to reproduce, at first. I had to concentrate till my eyes crossed to summon a wisp of light. But by the end of my third day in the apartment I could manage a ball of light almost as big as the one I had hurled at the Allacore commander. Trevyn never asked about my unusual power again, and when I tried to tell him about my practice, he just shrugged. I guess he figured he was better off not knowing.

That was when the headaches started. The first day I wrote it off to practicing too hard; after all I had summoned my biggest ball of light ever, and I had done it strictly through my own willpower. I was surprised when painkillers didn't help, but not unduly concerned. Typical stress headache, I told Trevyn, all I needed was a good night's sleep and I would be fine in the morning. He eyed my pale complexion dubiously but made no comment.

The second day was no better. My skull resonated with hammer blows from the inside out, my skin had all the color of pastry dough, and my eyes were surrounded by huge dark circles. I ached all over and I couldn't keep warm. When Trevyn came home for lunch, my sunken cheeks astonished him. My face had gone from merely sickly to downright skeletal over the course of a few hours. He skipped his afternoon classes and spoon-fed me soup at my bedside. When my eyes could no longer stand to have the lamp on, he spoon-fed me soup in the dark.

The third day I couldn't even get out of bed. Sitting up made me feel faint and dizzy, so I stopped trying. When Trevyn brought in the first soup of the day, I made a feeble attempt at humor and told him he should just hook me up to a soup IV. He didn't smile.

That afternoon the fever came. I soaked the sheets with sweat, and complained of the heat even with the fan on. My skin was on fire. I would no longer tolerate soup, and it agitated me so much that Trevyn quit trying to give it to me. By midnight I was having convulsions, and hallucinating. Trevyn told me I spent hours raving about Allacores, something he could only attribute to the attack a few days before. I thrashed around there on the bed, burning up with fever and unable to speak coherently, seeing things that weren't there, and Trevyn struggled with his dilemma. He was concerned for my health if he didn't take me to a hospital, and concerned for my safety if he did. In the end he made the difficult decision to keep me at the apartment. He draped me in damp towels, even wound my hair up in a wet towel on top of my head in a desperate attempt to bring my temperature down. He kept a wooden spoon by the bed for me to bite when I convulsed, and bathed my forehead with cool water while I hallucinated. And he prayed to a God many people found it hard to believe in since the Allacores came, and he wept when I finally fell asleep.

I woke up on the fifth morning. Trevyn slept in a chair beside the bed, his head slumped to one side at an angle that looked extremely uncomfortable. Towels covered me, stiff in that once-was-wet manner. I wanted to push them off of me, but I didn't even have the strength for that. In my weakened state, the frustration was more than I could handle, and hot tears slid down my face.

Trevyn jerked suddenly awake with a start, looking fearfully all around him. "Ellane? Are you alright? Where are you?" His wild gaze finally landed on me on the bed. "You're awake," he observed with surprise. "How are you feeling? Ellane, why are you crying?"

"I'm sorry," I sniffled, and managed to raise a hand to wipe at my tears. "I'm just so weak...."

He rubbed at his neck and leaned over, pulling towels off of me and piling them by the bed. "Honey, you've got to expect that. Do you realize how sick you were? You didn't know who I was--you didn't even know who you were."

Something in the way he said that rang flat. "What do you mean?"

Trevyn glanced at me sidelong. "You thought you were an Allacore," he said with a nervous laugh.

I sat there in stunned silence. I had thought I was an--Allacore? That was--was--unthinkable! Allacores were monsters, just monsters. I had more respect for the roaches that occasionally wandered into my bathroom than for Allacores. There was nothing in the world I despised more than Allacores. *Nothing.*

Trevyn took in the look on my face. "Don't look so upset. I know you're a xenophobe, but you were hallucinating, after all. Here, sit up a little and I'll take that towel out of your hair."

I struggled to cooperate, but in the end Trevyn put one arm behind me to hold me up, and used the other one to unwind the towel from my hair. I sighed in relief and flopped back on the pillows. Only then did I see the look on his face. "What? What's wrong?"

"Ellane....your hair...."

Panic gripped my throat. "What? What about my hair? Trevyn, talk to me!"

Without a word Trevyn reached over to the dresser and gave me a hand mirror. I took one last glance at his expression, and faced my reflection. The world seemed to stop, my gasp seemed to fill the room. The mirror fell from my hand.

My hair was white. Completely white, white like fresh-fallen snow. I looked up at Trevyn. He looked pretty much like I felt, like maybe we had both eaten too much cotton candy before getting on the tilt-a-whirl. "What happened to me?"

He shook his head slowly, picking the mirror up off the bed. "I don't know, Ellane. I don't know."

*****

In the aftermath of that traumatic discovery, I started down the long road to recovery. Trevyn fingered my hair and told me it was probably just some weird side effect of my illness that would reverse itself in time, but I couldn't bring myself to believe that. My hair was white--beyond blonde, and not at all like old people's white hair. Sitting alone with the hand mirror, I had to admit to myself that I had only seen hair like that one place before--on an Allacore.

A yawning pit opened in my stomach. I hated seeing any similarities at all between myself and those awful creatures, and I spent all morning working up the nerve to share my observation with Trevyn when he came home for lunch.

"Allacore hair?" He looked as shaken as I had been by the idea. "I don't know....I still say it's because you were sick. Why in the world would you suddenly have Allacore hair?"

I could feel the blood drain from my face. "Ohmigod....that's it. It was that device."

"What device?" Trevyn eyed me as if he feared I might start raving again.

"That telescope thing! That thing I used on the Allacore-- didn't she say it was going to take my power and give it to her?"

He sat down. "Oh, Lord. If that thing transfers power....and you left it on her until it killed her...."

"I don't know." I swallowed hard. "I don't know what would happen. Do you think that's why I got sick?"

He considered it. "Maybe. That, or something you transferred."

That conversation was enough to give me nightmares. I couldn't stop myself from reaching the inevitable conclusion--if the device transferred power, and I left it turned on the Allacore commander until she died, then along with whatever power I had received I had also received an Allacore's life force. And if I had transferred an Allacore's life force into myself, then white hair was probably the least of my troubles. But I didn't say anything more on the subject to Trevyn. In my mind, though, I kept a list of troubling new symptoms...

My hair stayed milky white. Over the course of the next few days, my eyes faded to a steely, intense gray that was almost metallic. Trevyn suggested uncertainly that the new color of my hair must have been making my eyes look different. All I could manage for a response to that was a strange smile. I ate normally, but my strength was very slow to return. My face was haunting and gaunt, and my whole body looked skeletally thin. When I finally could stand up out of bed, I was a full four inches taller than I had been--and I was almost six feet tall before! My cheekbones were higher, and more prominent. My fingers were noticeably longer. My ears were taking on a strange shape--almost as if they were trying to come to a point on top.

I faced myself in the mirror over the dresser one day, and realized with a chill that the traits that made me recognizably me were slipping away. Already my own mother would have had to look twice to know me--I would have had to look twice to know me.

I couldn't deny what was happening to me. These traits that were slowly making me unrecognizable were Allacore traits. The abyss yawned open in my stomach, and my hands were slick with cold sweat. Allacore traits! Was the Allacore life force I had absorbed slowly dominating my own? The Allacore invasion threatening the world as a whole was taking place on a more immediate scale in the details of my own face, the features of my own body. And as I looked into the steely Allacore eyes in the mirror that looked levelly back at me, I knew that Trevyn couldn't protect me from this. No one could protect me from this, and the consequences were sure to be disastrous to anyone who tried.

I knew what I had to do. I dug out my old canvas backpack and filled it with everything it would hold--a few changes of clothes, my wallet, toothbrush, toothpaste, hairbrush. I threw my makeup bag disdainfully back on the counter. What use had an Allacore for makeup? All the creams and powders on all the drugstore shelves in the world couldn't disguise the changes in me. Surely it would be the height of vanity to use makeup to try to make this face beautiful--my problems went far beyond how I looked. I stuffed a thin blanket into the bag and zipped it shut.

I knew I had to leave, but I had no idea where to go. I walked through the apartment one last time, trying to memorize every detail. I wished I could say goodbye to Trevyn, but I knew it was better this way. The less Trevyn knew about my situation, the better off he would be. He was scheduled to graduate at the end of this semester. With his political savvy and ambition, I knew he would go far--if he didn't have some half-human half-Allacore freak holding him back. I wiped the tears roughly off my face with a hand that felt too large to be mine, and locked the front door behind me.

*****

I didn't even look at a map; I just picked a road and followed it out of town. Sixteen miles later I came to a small town. Sixteen miles--hardly worth starting the car for, and it had taken me most of the day to get there. My feet had big puffy blisters, my face was sunburned, and I ached in places I hadn't known I had. At the first diner I came to I stopped.

The bells on the door jingled when I pushed it open, and a woman's voice from the back called, "Be right with you, honey." I tossed my backpack onto the bench seat of a booth, and edged myself in beside it. Vinyl red and white checked tablecloths covered the tables, and a neon clock advertising some beer or another hung over the counter. One of the neon letters was on the fritz, and buzzed on and off incessantly. It gave me a headache to watch it, so I looked away.

The woman who came to the table had hair dyed so red it had a pink cast to it, and her lipstick was very red indeed. The crow's feet by her eyes told a story that her pancaked makeup couldn't hide. Her name was embroidered in blue thread on her pink uniform dress: "LaVerne." She smiled at me, though, and her smile seemed genuine. "What'll it be, hon?"

I hadn't even glanced at the menu--I probably couldn't afford half of what was on there anyway. The few dollars I had in my wallet had to last me indefinitely now. What on earth had I gotten myself into? "Do you have grilled cheese?" I said at last, uncertainly.

"Course. You have anything to drink?"

"Just water," I said softly, for some insane reason embarrassed by my order.

"Sure thing. I'll have that out for you in a sec, hon." She ripped the top sheet off her order pad and slipped her pen behind her ear, turning back toward the kitchen. "Got a big spender here for you, Charlie," I heard her say. She clipped the order onto the string stretched above the length of the counter.

I sighed and picked up a packet of sugar, playing with it idly. My situation was a good deal worse than I wanted to admit, even to myself. I had nowhere to sleep, very little money, and no way to earn more. What was I going to do?

I toyed with the sugar packet, but it was offering no answers.

I had arrived at no great conclusions when LaVerne brought

my meal; a grilled cheese sandwich cut into triangles on a chipped plate piled high with broken potato chips. She set my water down beside the plate. It was in a big plastic cup that said "Enjoy Coke" in very faded white lettering, and it had a slice of lemon stuck on the edge. "Here you go, sugar," she said. "Need anything else?"

I hesitated, considering all of the things I might tell her, and finally shook my head. "No, thanks, this looks great." It was the truth. The sandwich was my first meal that day, and it looked great.

I ate in contemplative silence, turning my options over in my mind. I couldn't go back to Trevyn's without endangering him; I couldn't let him take that risk. I had to stand on my own. But I was almost out of money, and I had no place to stay. I was going to have to find a job, first of all. After I had a source of income, I could worry about finding somewhere to stay. It would overwhelm me if I tried to worry about everything at once.

Before I realized it, I had cleaned the plate, and drained the last of my water. As if the clatter of the ice in the empty cup was a signal, LaVerne appeared at the table. "How was everything? You need some more water?" She held the pitcher ready by the cup.

"Um--no, thanks. It was great." I hesitated as she gathered my plate and cup. "I'm new here, and....do--do you know where I might find some work?"

She eyed me a moment, the place and cup in one hand and the pitcher of ice water in the other. A large drop of condensation gathered on the bottom of the pitcher, and fell to the floor while she considered me. I watched it, fighting an urge to squirm under that silent gaze.

"I'm probably crazy," she said finally. "I don't know you from Adam, and it's plain that you've got trouble. But for some crazy reason I feel like I should help you." She shifted the pitcher in her grasp as if it was straining her wrist. "Lord knows we could use the help. Charlie and me, we run this place ourselves, you know. Was easier when we were younger, but now....well, I could really use another pair of hands to help me out around here."

I stared at her, afraid to believe what I was hearing. "You'd let me work here--for you?"

She shrugged, curbing the gesture short before she slopped water out of the pitcher. "Call me crazy. Like I said, we need the help."

Flustered, I scrambled around in my backpack for my wallet. "I--thank you....how much do I owe you?"

She gestured derisively with the water pitcher. "On the house. Look, I know it ain't my place to say, but it's plain you're on hard times. Charlie and me, we were on hard times too once...." She trailed off for a second. "Anyway, point is, there's a little room back of the diner. It isn't much, but it's a bed when you're sleepy, and a shower when you're dirty."

I was flabbergasted. And I couldn't help but wonder if she would have taken me in if she had known what I was, what I had done. "I--I can't thank you enough," I said, as clearly as I was able. "You're very kind."

"And you're very tired." LaVerne waved that pitcher my direction again. "Why don't you go ahead to the back and get yourself settled in...." she paused expectantly, and I realized that I had never told her my name.

"Ellane," I said, cramming my wallet back into my backpack and zipping it shut. "Ellane Williams.

She nodded in my direction. "I'm LaVerne Spencer. My husband Charlie is the cook, I expect you'll see him tomorrow. We open at six. See you then?"

"With bells on," I assured her, smiling in spite of myself.

And so I worked at Charlie's Diner, six a.m. to ten p.m. every day except Sunday, when we were closed. The hours were long, the work was tiring, and the pay was minimal, but I was more grateful than I could say. The little room behind the diner was my haven, and in the cloudy mirror over the bathroom counter, I watched the disconcerting changes in myself continue.

My thick, white hair grew unbelievably fast--it was already halfway down my back. I wore it pulled up under a hairnet at work, and no one seemed to notice its incredible color. But the worst shock came when I went to wash my face one evening. When I stuck my hands under the running water, there were no fingernails on my fingers! The tips of my fingers were forming deep cracks in them, like you might expect in the middle of winter when your skin was too dry. I bought a pair of crocheted lace gloves at a thrift store and wore them constantly to cover my hands. What could I do? I was inexorably becoming that which I hated most.

Toward the end of my second week at the diner, a stranger in a dark suit came in early for dinner. He wore dark sunglasses even indoors, and carried a black leather briefcase that stayed on the table while he ate. He regarded me from behind those sunglasses with a long, steady gaze that made me acutely uncomfortable. I took his order and stayed away from his table, but I could still feel that prickly gaze burning into my back as I worked. I dropped his strip steak dinner on the table with a clatter, and backed a step away from him. "Anything else?"

"No, no, this looks fine. I'm famished," he said, ignoring the food. He barreled on with his one-sided conversation before I could retreat to the kitchen. "I'm on my way back to DC--I've been investigating an Allacore incident over at the university."

"Really?" I croaked. My hands felt clammy.

"Sure enough, and who would have thought such a thing would happen way the hell out here? That Trevyn Blaine, though, he handled it exceptionally well. I guess you've probably heard of him, everyone has by now. A real hero."

I nodded numbly. What was he doing? How could I get out of this conversation?

"That's actually the reason they sent me," he continued conversationally, nailing me to the spot with that dispassionate stare. "The President is very interested in him; in fact he's already been flown out to Washington for some interviews. Someone like that could go far right now, politically speaking."

"That's wonderful," I said, "but I really don't--"

"But I found some other things, too." He was still staring at me, speaking exactly as though I had not said a word. "According to several eyewitnesses, it wasn't Trevyn Blaine who defeated the Allacore at all. They say there was a woman there, who has since left town."

Enough was enough. Whatever he was doing, I wanted no part of it, and I no longer cared about politeness. I turned away, determined to go to the kitchen. I wasn't coming back out until this menacing stranger left.

Faster than I could follow, his hand shot out and clamped around my wrist, and jerked me back to the table. I cried out, more in surprise than pain, and turned to find him standing there.

"Hey, now!" The shout came from Charlie in the kitchen, watching over the counter. "There'll be no mishandling of the waitresses, mister. You can just take your fancy-suit-wearin' ass on down the road!"

The stranger paid no attention. "They say she fought the

Allacore with summoned balls of light," he hissed at me. "They say she's some kind of freak. And they say she came this way."

I was soaked with cold sweat. I was frightened--and I was angry. Who was this self-important little man to say such things to me? *Freak?*

I didn't realize until I felt the stinging in my fingertips what was about to happen. And before I could stop it, gleaming white talons tore through my gloves.

He jumped back from me. "I knew it!" His composure was finally rattled, and that pleased me. I held my hands defensively in front of me, brandishing my talons at him. They were as sharp as razors and incredibly strong, and he eyed them warily. "What the hell are you?"

A distinctive sound registered over my ragged breathing, loud in the silent diner--the sound of someone cocking a shotgun. With a feral growl, I whirled around.

LaVerne stood in the doorway to the kitchen, holding the gun in both hands. Incredibly, she wasn't aiming it at me.

"You best get on out of here, stranger. I don't know what you've come here for and I don't care, but we don't let nobody attack our waitresses."

"Attack?" He looked from LaVerne to me, incredulous. "Are you crazy, lady? It isn't me waving talons at her!"

LaVerne shook her head. "Charlie and me saw you harassing her. Seems to me you're lucky she didn't do more than just wave them. Now you'd just better get your fanny on up the road, mister. Now."

We stood in silence for several uncomfortable seconds after he left. LaVerne lowered the gun with shaking hands. "Ellane, what's happened to you?"

I shook my head, fighting back tears. "It doesn't matter. And

24

it's probably better if you don't know. I'll go back to my room now. I'll be gone in the morning."

"But Ellane, we can help you!"

"No." I turned for the door. "No one can help me. I'm sorry. But I can't let you put yourself in danger for me. I'll leave tonight."

I went into my little room, locked the door, and leaned against it.

I was alone again.

*****

So I left Charlie's Diner, alone and on foot, before the sun rose. LaVerne had left my wages in an envelope slipped under the door, so I had a little money to take with me. It lasted me through a week of aimless wandering from town to town. I was mentally lost--I didn't know where I should go or what I should do. I knew that I couldn't let anyone get close to me, and so I didn't.

I was homeless and I looked it. All I owned was what I hauled around in my backpack. My few clothes and myself I cleaned in streams and ponds. I still wore my lace gloves to cover my fingers; they were ragged and had holes where my talons had torn through, but they sufficed. I attracted odd glances, but nobody really suspected what I was. Large hands and white hair did not necessarily mean Allacore, and I could hide the talons. Things were rough, but bearable.

Until the morning I woke up and found my wings had sprouted.

I was sleeping under a bench in a city park, beside a lake. I leaned over the lake with my wings spread and looked at my reflection, and cried. I cried because I was growing farther and farther away from myself, I cried because those white-feathered wings were things of such beauty, yet so unwanted, I cried because I was tired and hungry and the weather was turning cold. But most of all I cried because I wanted my life back, and I could never have it.

When my tears finally subsided, I tried to think rationally. I needed some way to cover these things. The t-shirt I was wearing was ruined; it had torn open in the back. No blouse was going to cover those things; I was going to have to cut anything I wore to let them out. But where was I going to find anything to hide them? I couldn't venture into a store, not with these wings. I had no money anyway. I had nothing to bargain for, and nobody to bargain with. I had nothing to eat and nowhere to sleep. I had a body I didn't recognize, and not a friend to my name.

I had a lake in front of me, and the tempting thought of throwing myself in.

The thought of escape loomed in front of me like a dark abyss, dizzying to contemplate. I had been through so much in the last few weeks--for a little while, kneeling there at the edge of that lake, my control crumbled and I felt terribly sorry for myself. Sorry enough, for a moment, to end it all.

A hiccup from the dirt path caught my attention, and I looked up to see a man swaggering by. The sun was barely up, but this fellow had obviously already been hitting the sauce. He clutched a paper bag in his right hand, and he made his unsteady way down the red dirt path on sandals. He was wearing a black cloak that trailed along on the ground behind him.

I grabbed my bag and ran to catch up with him, praying my t-shirt was still in one piece enough to hold. He stood and regarded me, swaying slightly in the morning sun. "Well, what have we here," he said. "Looks like one of them Allashores. G'morning, missy."

"Good morning," I said.

"What's good about it?" he demanded, his mood abruptly changing. "This damn sun is hurting my eyes, not warming my bones. My feet's cold."

"Well," I said carefully, not wanting to precipitate another mood swing, "that could be because you are wearing sandals. What you need are some warmer shoes."

He didn't anger. Instead, he became mournful. "Ah, yes, some warm shoes. Can't, though. Got no money."

"Well," I said again, "I have some sneakers here that might work. Would you be willing to trade for, say, your cloak?"

He brightened. "This old thing? Sure, sure....show me the shoes."

I pulled my Reeboks out of my bag and gave them to him. I had bought them at a thrift store to fit my feet, which had grown as oversized as my hands. The sneakers were an oddly large size, and they were almost new. But they had almost immediately become too small, and the hide on my feet was tough enough now I generally went barefoot. He whistled. "These are nice, missy, real nice. Nicer than this old cloak. You sure you want to trade?"

I shrugged. "I don't need the shoes. I could use a cloak."

"Done." He handed me the cloak, and sat down to put on his sneakers. I was pleased to see that they fit him; at least as well as the sandals had. I didn't want to feel like I had cheated a homeless drunk just because he was the only person who would possibly deal with me.

*****

With the cloak covering my torn shirts and feathered wings, I felt much less conspicuous, even though people still recognized me easily enough for what I was. I wandered for another couple of days, avoiding people completely, until my hunger got the best of me. Allacores, I knew, would kill an animal and eat it raw, but I would not stoop to that level. At the edge of a town, I found a little pastel blue house with lace curtains showing in the windows, and neatly kept window boxes with pansies growing in them. The pastel blue reminded me of the curtains in my old room at Trevyn's apartment, and for no better reason than that, I decided to try it.

There was no answer when I knocked on the door. I cautiously tried the knob. It turned, so I pushed the door open and stepped inside with some trepidation. No one was in sight, but I could hear old-timey piano music drifting in from the hallway to the left, so that was the direction I started. "Hello? Is anyone home?"

The white-haired lady that peeked around the corner at me should have been someone's grandmother, if she wasn't. The bespectacled eyes widened as they took me in, but instead of the shriek I expected, she just swallowed hard, and held an arm out toward me. "Come on in," she said, her voice quavering only a little. "You must be starved. I'm sure we have something in here somewhere that you would like to eat. I made some vegetable soup for my son's visit. You are welcome to it."

I was more than a little surprised--this was the first person who had shown me kindness since LaVerne. I followed her into the small kitchen, where she was already ladling steaming soup into a chipped bowl. "You mean you--you aren't afraid of me?" She was the first person I had met in days who hadn't run screaming from me or tried to kill me outright, and I was grateful for her hospitality.

She glanced at me from the corner of her eyes as she placed the bowl in front of me. "Of course I'm afraid of you, dear--truth be told I'm scared half to death. But if you wanted to do me harm, you certainly wouldn't have come in like you did. You had plenty of chance. And you look like you haven't eaten decently in days. I don't know how much help I can be, but I can offer you something to fill your belly." *Something other than me,* her wide eyes told me.

Resisting a strong urge to bury my face in the bowl--something that would surely only strengthen the fear she was so obviously fighting against--I reached for the tablespoon she had brought with the soup. It was unexpectedly unfamiliar, and I fumbled with it, trying to get my clumsy fingers around it. It was frustrating and embarrassing, and tears burned at the backs of my eyes. I finally gave up and wrapped my hand around the handle in a fist--I was determined not to eat like the creature I was coming to resemble.

She watched me struggle with the spoon, and I tried not to notice her watching. I ducked my head to hide my angry tears, and so I was startled to feel her hand fall on my shoulder. I looked up at her in surprise, and she looked down at me with undisguised sympathy. "You poor dear," she said softly. "I don't know what's happened to you, but you haven't always been like this, have you?"

I shook my head, blinking back more unexpected tears at her kindness. Concentrating, I tried to dip the spoon in the soup to eat, and ended up slopping some out of the bowl. This was so damned frustrating! I had the motor skills of a toddler--I couldn't control my own hands enough to eat soup from a spoon! I moaned and tried again.

The grandmotherly lady brought me a linen napkin. She placed it beside my bowl with a hand that shook slightly from age and fear--not clumsiness, like me. "I don't want to upset you, dear," she said hesitantly, "but maybe that would be easier for you if you drink it from the bowl."

"Like an animal?" I cried in anguish.

She sat down across the table from me. "No, not like an animal--like a person. Didn't you ever drink your milk from the cereal bowl when you were a child?"

It was getting hard to remember what it had been like to be a child. I nodded uncertainly. "Yes," I said, and as I said it, I really could remember. "Yes, I did."

"I still do," she said conspiratorially. "You don't have to eat like an animal--or like an Allacore. You can be perfectly civilized without using that spoon that's giving you fits."

I liked this lady more by the minute. "Thank you," I said hoarsely, and I meant it. She had shown me how to retain my dignity when I thought there was no chance. I cupped my hands carefully around the bowl, mindful that with my still unaccustomed brute strength I could easily break it, and drank deeply of the hot soup. I could feel it all the way down to my belly, which grumbled in gratitude. I drank again, and emptied the bowl by half.

My first meal in days completely occupied my attention. I never heard the approaching footsteps. The first clue I had that someone else was in the house was the cold barrel of the gun pressed against my temple. "Get up, Allacore."

My talons snapped out in my sudden fear, shattering the bowl and spilling soup all over the table and me. "Ronald!" the lady gasped. "Put that thing away! Get out of here!"

"I said get up, Allacore!" Ronald apparently had no intention of obeying. I rose from the table, slowly, so he wouldn't freak out and shoot me.

The grandmotherly lady stood too. "Ronald, please! This young lady is my guest. Let her eat, she's--"

"This is no one's guest, Mother. She's an Allacore!"

"No, she isn't." She held her hands out to her son, attempting to placate him. "Please, put down the gun. This girl is human!"

"Human?" The gun ground into my temple. "She's the one they are looking for--the one from the university!"

"Wait," I said, starting to turn around. "I'll go, there's no--"

"Don't move. I'll shoot you where you stand, I swear it. You're not leaving here until the police take you away."

His mother sank into her chair. "You called the police? Oh, Ronald. What have you done?"

I could hear the cars squealing into the driveway already. "Honestly, Mother, I don't understand you." He was unapologetic. "This woman is dangerous. I know you've heard the news reports--and I find you in here eating with her?"

Like something out of a nightmare, police officers swarmed into the room, guns drawn. They surrounded me and herded me out; my last view of the house was of Ronald's mother, sitting in her chair shaking her head and moaning, "Oh, Ronald" over and over.

*****

If I had felt things were bad the morning I sat by the lake and thought about drowning, it was only because I had not realized how much worse they could still have been. Sitting alone in the cold, dark jail cell, I began to get a feeling for what bad really was. I had not heard any of the news reports Ronald had mentioned, so I had no idea what these policemen must have heard about me, but their opinions were clear enough. They taunted me, humiliated me, and denied me the basic rights of food and privacy. And who would care? It was clear enough that to them I was public enemy number one.

I sat there in that cell, in the dark that seemed to my Allacore eyes as bright as daylight, and thought about everything that had happened to me in the past weeks. I looked at my gloves, at my cloak, at my bare, tough feet, and thought about all that I was hiding.

I pulled off the gloves, and extended my talons. I had only recently learned how to do that consciously, and oddly enough, I was proud of the skill. Holding out my hands, I watched the moonlight from the single barred window play across the surfaces of my talons, surprised to find that I thought it beautiful. And they were my talons--no longer strange after the weeks I had spent with them. I had found them surprisingly useful on occasions, from scaring away the government agent in Charlie's Diner, to digging holes, to cutting twine.

I dropped my cloak and spread my wings. There almost wasn't room to extend them fully in the small cell, but it felt undeniably good to stretch them. Perhaps I wasn't doing myself any favors keeping them curled up all the time, trying to hide what everyone knew. In the moonlight, the feathers had a soft glow. I reached around and stroked at them. They were soft! I had spent so much time trying to deny the changes I had gone through, I had never even noticed the feathers on my wings had such a wonderful texture. And those feet--there was something to be said for the ability to wander the wild barefoot.

Somehow, even though I wished these changes had never happened, they had come to be a part of my definition of me. As the grandmotherly lady in the blue house had shown me, it was possible to have these Allacore features and still be very human. Which made me wonder about the Allacores themselves. They had shown up literally out of the blue three months ago, attacking and raiding and capturing. Why? I had never before concerned myself with their motives, being too busy despising them on a gut level that had nothing to do with their actions. Trevyn had been right. I was a xenophobe.

Revelation struck me like lightning, that I could change so much and yet still be me. In that new light, I wondered why my first response had been to run away. That in turn brought me to another realization: I couldn't do this alone. I had been trying, and failing, to handle it on my own for a month now. Every time someone tried to help me, I ran away--from Trevyn, from LaVerne, from others I had never even given a chance. On my own, I could never hope to be more than I was right now; a fugitive running from town to town, frightening folks who didn't know any better. I needed friends--I needed a "normal" person to vouch for me that other people would trust, to make the world take a closer look at me. And from there, who knew what I might be able to do? I was really in a unique position to be of help with the Allacore situation, it finally occurred to me, because of the metamorphosis I had undergone. I was no longer completely human, nor was I completely Allacore, but somewhere in the middle. I was something that both sides could relate to, which was something that had been missing.

Until now. In an odd way, being in jail was the best thing that had happened to me since I left Trevyn's apartment a month ago. For the first time I could look past my loss and see the possibilities. For the first time I was master of my own destiny. And for the first time I knew clearly where I was headed.

I was going back to Trevyn Blaine.

That night, I did something I had not done for four weeks. I concentrated, and summoned a ball of light. Standing as far away

33

as I could, with my back pressed against the bars, I hurled it at the outside wall of the cell.

Jail cells were built tough, but they were not built to withstand miniature suns. A gaping, smoldering hole had opened in the wall, taking a good portion of the ceiling of my cell with it. The noise probably awakened the whole town, but I didn't care. Before the dust had begun to settle, I was gone.

*****

"Ellane!" Trevyn's gasp was involuntary, the joy on his face genuine. I had worried about what sort of reception I might receive, how his feelings might have changed after I left without a word. I had worried enough that, though I had located his new apartment within two hours of arriving in Washington DC, I had waited until almost midnight to actually ring the doorbell. If he had turned against me, I wanted to be able to escape.

But apparently I needn't have worried. Despite the late hour, he was dressed and seemed awake, and the lights in the apartment were on. He hugged me hard and pulled me inside.

"I can't believe it's really you! Oh, Ellane, when I saw the news reports about your escape, I knew you would be coming. I don't know how, but I knew. Sit down, I'll get you something to eat, to drink. Things must have been rough for you."

"Thank you," I said, and sat down on the couch. I had no idea what to say to him. I had not even begun to sort it out when he came back from the kitchen, with a cold cut sandwich and a glass of wine. "Oh, thank you," I said again. The trip to DC had not been as hard for me as the month before it, because I knew at last where I was going, but I had still been a fugitive, eating only what I could find, where I could find it. That sandwich was the best thing I had seen in days.

He waited until I was halfway through it to say anything. "I should shoot you, you know, for running out like you did. Are you alright?"

I looked up at him in surprise. "Are you kidding? Trevyn, you are special advisor to the President on the Allacore situation. Do you think you would have gotten here with me by your side?"

He glowered at me. "Do you think I would have cared?"

"I'm sorry," I said, humbled. "I was doing what I thought was best. I didn't want to endanger you."

"I know. But you haven't answered me. Are you alright?"

I finished eating and sat back on the couch. "As alright as I will ever be. I am not the same as I used to be. But that's okay."

He beamed at me. "I never thought I would hear you say that. I was worried that you would never accept what had happened. Honestly, Ellane, I was afraid you had left to do away with yourself."

I laughed uncomfortably, brushing away the thought of a time when I had considered just that. "Listen, Trevyn, there is another reason why I had to find you. I want to help with the Allacore situation. Does anyone have any idea why they are invading us?"

He looked at me curiously. "No. We haven't had much success getting them to talk with us. All we can assume is that they want the planet, and have no particular compunctions against removing us to get it."

I shook my head. "I don't know. I think we need to find out. Until we know why they are doing what they are, we don't really know if we have a hope of negotiating with them."

"Negotiating? You really have changed. How do you propose to get them to talk to us?"

"Me," I said simply. "Has it ever occurred to you that I might not be the only xenophobe you've been dealing with?"

Trevyn goggled at me. "You're right. It's that simple. They won't talk to us for the same reason they attack us--whatever that is. You--you are similar enough to them that you might stand a chance of getting them to talk to you." He slapped the arm of the chair he was sitting in. "That's brilliant!"

I smiled and batted my eyelashes at him. "Of course. Some things have not changed."

*****

Within days, I was at the Pentagon, sitting in an uncomfortable straight-backed chair in front of a television camera. With Trevyn on my side, it was amazing how quickly the charges against me were resolved. With his testimony about what had happened at the university, and LaVerne's account of the incident at Charlie's Diner, and my idea about communicating with the Allacores through me, the justice system was more than happy to overlook the jail building I had damaged in my escape.

So now I faced the blinking red light above the camera's lens that meant our broadcast was live. This was sent on every frequency possible, in the hopes that the Allacore would receive one of them. Could they even receive television broadcasts? We didn't know. We could only hope.

"Men and women of the Allacore," I said, "we of Earth send greetings. I am contacting you this day to ask for communication. I know that you do not wish to talk to the humans. I ask you instead to talk to me. You know who I am; you know what I am. I am willing to meet on whatever terms you name. If this proposal is acceptable, contact us however you wish and name your terms. I will meet them."

The broadcast was run three times, then the airways were cleared for twenty minutes to await any possible response. The

36

pattern was then repeated. We couldn't force them to listen, we couldn't force them to answer.

All we could do was wait.

*****

Trevyn shook me out of a sound sleep that night. "Wh--what?" I stammered, flustered. "What happened?" I caught sight of the red glowing digits of the alarm clock as I sat up in bed. 2:34 am.

"Hurry and get dressed," he said. "It's the Allacore."

"Oh!" I was out of bed in an instant, and dressed almost as fast. I followed him out into the hallway. "I'm sorry, I didn't hear the phone. Do we need to leave right away?"

He cast a strange look over his shoulder at me.

In the living room were three Allacores, two females and one male, standing awkwardly in the middle of the room. "Oh," I said weakly, finally understanding.

"Greetings, Ellane," one of the women said. "We have accepted your offer to communicate. I am Commander Gretasa. This is Commander Sothe, and Commodore Liasa."

"I am honored," I said. Commander Gretasa wore her white hair plaited in long braids that hung down her back. She wore leather armor, and gold earrings. I had never seen an Allacore wear jewelry before. I wondered how many other things about them I had never guessed. Commander Sothe stood slightly behind the two females, also in leather armor. He had a long scar that ran from his right temple down to the corner of his mouth.

Commodore Liasa was easily the tallest of the three. She wore bright silver armor, and had her hair cut short, though not as short as the commander I had encountered. Her eyes were bright and intelligent.

"Would you like to sit?" I gestured at the couch. It wasn't a brilliant opener, but I didn't know what else to say, and I wanted to be as polite as I could. If there was any chance of stopping this hopeless war, I was sure it would have to come from this meeting.

"Thank you, no." Commodore Liasa was gracious, but firm. "Your offer of dialogue intrigued us. Though we know you are essentially human, I must admit that we find it easier to converse with someone who looks as one of our own."

"I can understand that," I said truthfully. "I wanted to discuss any possibility that may exist of peacefully resolving this dispute. You may not be aware of it, but we actually have no idea why you have attacked us."

"We attacked you?" Commander Gretasa sounded honestly shocked. "The humans began this dispute. We have only brought it back to your planet."

"What?" I glanced at Trevyn, but he seemed as confused as I was. "Our hyperdrive ship Intrepid was lost, and we have not judged it worth the risk to try again."

"Lost?" Liasa leaned closer. "Intrepid was not lost. We destroyed it."

Trevyn's gasp echoed my feelings, but I did my best to remain neutral in my response. "I don't understand."

The Commodore began to pace across the small living room. "Intrepid came out of hyperspace near our home planet. They landed there, without contacting us, without our permission. Our fathers asked them to leave." She shrugged. "I know the humans have a low opinion of us, Ellane, but all we desire, all we ever desired, was to be left alone. The Intrepid ignored our request, claiming that their situation was such that they had no choice. They had a dying crewman, they said, they must find medical assistance."

38

"That sounds excusable," I said carefully.

"Does it?" Liasa was obviously trying hard to keep her temper in check. "I suppose it would, until one considers that this human was dying of a human disease! Allacores had never been exposed to this illness, had no immunity to it, no defense against it--it decimated our planet. Half of our people died. Those who survived built a ship--our ship--and started toward Earth. They knew the journey was too long to make in a lifetime--or several. But what was there to stay for? They left for vengeance against the human barbarians. Now we, their descendants, have arrived to take it."

"Oh, my Lord." I sat down heavily. "I--I don't know what to say. I don't know how I can plead our innocence to you. You've been raised to hate us."

"No. We have been raised to hate those with no honor. Landing a ship with an alien disease on a thriving planet was a dishonorable action. Did it mean the entire planet the ship came from was dishonorable? We did not know. But when we arrived here, we were fired upon. There was no contact, no attempts to communicate or to discover our purpose. If we had reacted similarly to Intrepid, our planet might have been spared its destruction. But to attack a traveler unprovoked is an action without honor. When some of our people were sent to the surface of your planet to seek dialogue, they were spurned and attacked before they could even speak. These are actions without honor. What could we then assume, but that the entire planet was like this?"

I shook my head. "These actions were not motivated by blind hate, Commodore. These people acted out of fear. Fear may be a product of ignorance, but it is not dishonorable. To some, it would seem dishonorable to seek vengeance on people many generations removed from those who did you harm."

Liasa seemed surprised. "That is a more logical argument than I expected to hear from a human." She glanced at her companions. "We should leave you now. You have given us much to consider. I must admit we thought of humans as savages, monsters. We weren't sure the concept of honor would even be understood here. Our basis for this war may need to be reconsidered. It seems we have some matters to discuss with regard to our vengeance, and whether it is justified. We shall need more communication, and we shall need it with a larger group of those in command. Will that be possible?"

"Absolutely." I managed to wait until after they had left to do a victory dance. Contrary to my earlier beliefs, this was an intelligent and logical opponent, and I felt certain that such an enemy could be reasoned with. A dispute that began over a misunderstanding did not need to continue that way if both sides were willing to talk. I was humbled to find that the attitude I had once held toward Allacores was identical to the one they held about me!

Once, when the world around me was chaos, my own life reflected that chaos in terrifying ways. I had fought changes I could not control, I had tried to be an island, and nearly killed myself doing it. What couldn't be changed must be accepted. I knew that now, and that knowledge had helped me to end my own suffering, and possibly heal a larger hurt as well. Now that I had brought my life into balance again, it seemed perhaps the world around me was ready to follow my lead.

Sign up to receive notifications of new releases

www.eepurl.com/tP5NP

Connect with me online:

www.sandra-miller.com